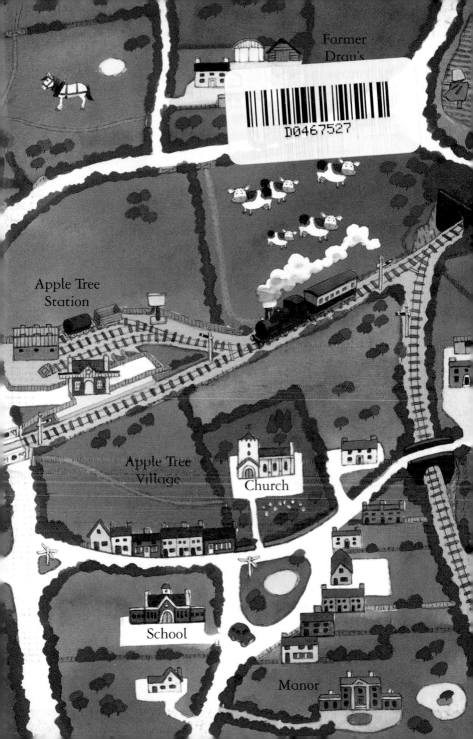

Farmer Drau's

Apple Tree
Station

Apple Tree
Village

Church

School

Manor

Farmyard Tales

Kitten's Day Out

Heather Amery

Adapted by Rob Lloyd Jones

Illustrated by Stephen Cartwright

Reading consultant: Alison Kelly

Find the duck on every double page.

This story is about Apple Tree Farm,

Sam,

Poppy,

Mrs. Boot,

Ted,

Mr. Bran

and Fluff, the kitten.

It was a busy day on
Apple Tree Farm.

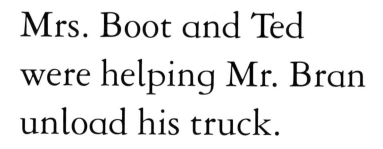

Mrs. Boot and Ted
were helping Mr. Bran
unload his truck.

Sam was playing
with Fluff.

Mr. Bran drove away.
"Goodbye!" Poppy
waved.

"Where's Fluff?"
asked Sam.

"She's not in the shed,"
said Ted.

"She's not outside,"
said Poppy.

"Did she jump into
Mr. Bran's truck?"
asked Mrs. Boot.

"We have to get her!"
said Sam.

But which way did
Mr. Bran go?

9

Ted drove down a hill.

The car splashed into
a stream.

Ted had to push
the car out.

"I hope we can still find
Mr. Bran," Sam said.

They set off again.
Now there were sheep
on the road.

Ted honked the horn
until the sheep moved.

Honk!

Honk!

At last they
spotted a truck.

"Look!" said Poppy. "Is that Mr. Bran's truck?"

But it was the
wrong truck.

It was getting late, so
they drove home.

"We'll never find poor
Fluff," Sam sighed.

There was a surprise waiting at Apple Tree Farm.

"Fluff!" cried Sam.

Mr. Bran had brought
her back.

Sam smiled and
hugged his kitten.

"We'll never lose you again," he promised.

Puzzles

Puzzle 1

Put the five pictures in order.

A.

B.

C.

D.

E.

Puzzle 2

Can you spot six differences between these two pictures?

Puzzle 3

Who's who? Match the names to the people or animals in this story.

 Mr. Bran

Sam

 Mrs. Boot

Poppy

Fluff

Ted

Puzzle 4

Choose the right sentence for each picture.

A.

Mr. Bran drove away.

Mr. Bran ran away.

B.

"She's not in the bed."

"She's not in the shed."

C.

Ted drove down a hill.
Ted ran up a hill.

D.

Ted had to push the car out.
Ted had to lift the car up.

Answers to puzzles
Puzzle 1

1D.

2C.

3B.

4A.

5E.

Puzzle 2

Puzzle 3

Poppy

Sam

Fluff

Mr. Bran

Ted

Mrs. Boot

Puzzle 4

A. Mr. Bran drove away.

B. "She's not in the shed."

C. Ted drove down a hill.

D. Ted had to push the car out.

Designed by Laura Nelson
Series editor: Lesley Sims
Series designer: Russell Punter
Digital manipulation by
Nick Wakeford and John Russell

This edition first published in 2016 by Usborne Publishing Ltd.,
Usborne House, 83-85 Saffron Hill, London EC1N 8RT, England.
www.usborne.com Copyright © 2016, 1992 Usborne Publishing Ltd.

USBORNE FIRST READING
Level Two

USBORNE FIRST READING
Farmyard Tales
The Silly Sheepdog
Illustrated by
Stephen Cartwright

USBORNE FIRST READING
Farmyard Tales
The Runaway Tractor
Illustrated by
Stephen Cartwright

USBORNE FIRST READING
Farmyard Tales
The Naughty Sheep
Illustrated by
Stephen Cartwright

Farmyard Tales
Tractor in Trouble
Illustrated by
Stephen Cartwright

USBORNE FIRST READING
Farmyard Tales
Market Day
Illustrated by
Stephen Cartwright

USBORNE FIRST READING
Farmyard Tales
The New Pony
Illustrated by
Stephen Cartwright

USBORNE FIRST READING
Farmyard Tales
Pig Gets Lost

USBORNE FIRST READING
Farmyard Tales
Woolly Stops the Train
Illustrated by
Stephen Cartwright

Farmyard Tales
Camping Out
Illustrated by
Stephen Cartwright